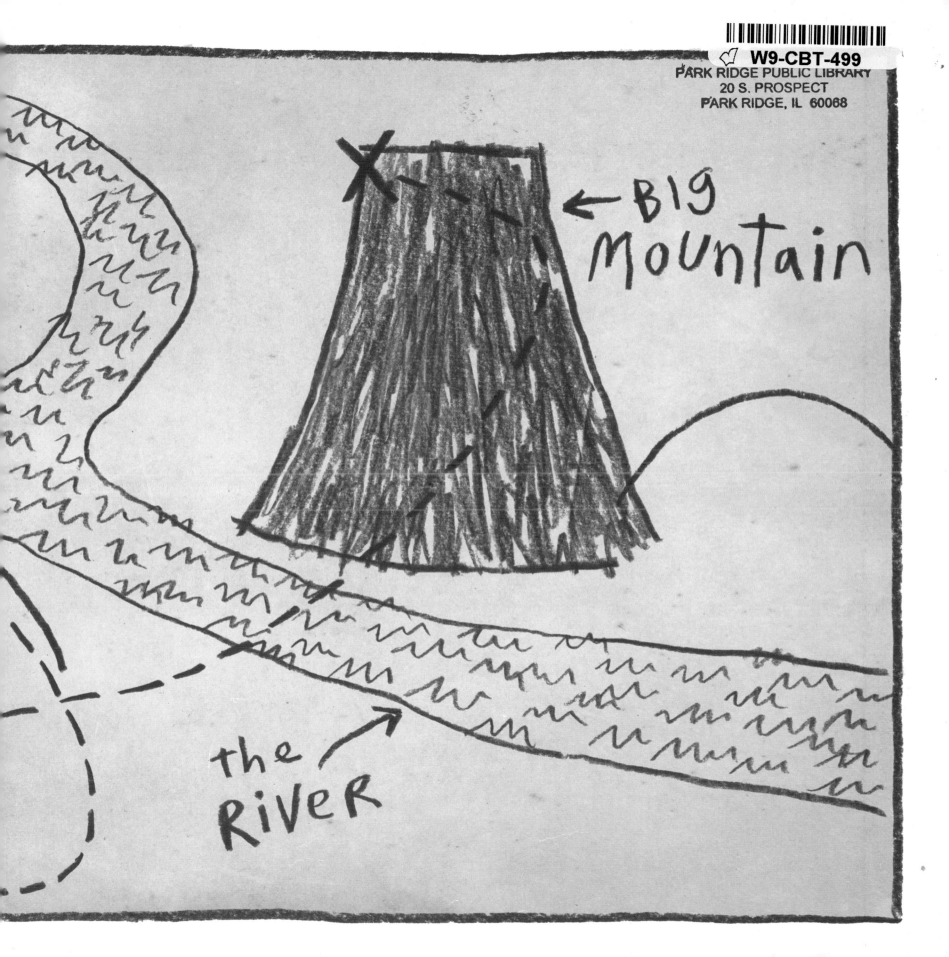

TO MY FAVORITE DAUGHTER DINOSAUR AND DADDY DINOSAUR.
I LOVE YOU, LUCY AND BRIAN!—L. B.

FOR JEANNE CLARK—B. C.

SIMON & SCHUSTER BOOKS FOR YOUNG READERS

An imprint of Simon & Schuster Children's Publishing Division

1230 Avenue of the Americas, New York, New York 10020

Text copyright © 1997 by Laurie Berkner

Illustrations copyright © 2017 by Ben Clanton

SIMON & SCHUSTER BOOKS FOR YOUNG READERS is a trademark of Simon & Schuster, Inc.

For information about special discounts for bulk purchases, please contact Simon & Schuster Special Sales

at 1-866-506-1949 or business@simonandschuster.com.

The Simon & Schuster Speakers Bureau can bring authors to your live event. For more information or to book an event,

contact the Simon & Schuster Speakers Bureau at 1-866-248-3049 or visit our website at www.simonspeakers.com.

Book design by Lucy Ruth Cummins

The text for this book was set in Fratello Nick.

The illustrations for this book were rendered in colored pencil, acrylic paint, and watercolor, and were assembled in Adobe Photoshop.

Manufactured in the United States of America

0317 PCH

2 4 6 8 10 9 7 5 3

Library of Congress Cataloging-in-Publication Data

Names: Berkner, Laurie, author. | Clanton, Ben, 1988- illustrator.

Title: We are the dinosaurs / Laurie Berkner ; illustrated by Ben Clanton.

Description: First edition. | New York : Simon & Schuster Books for Young Readers, [2017] | Summary: Dinosaurs eat, rest,

roar, and march, making the earth flat.

Identifiers: LCCN 2015032132 |

ISBN 9781481464635 (hardcover : alk. paper) | ISBN 9781481464642 (eBook)

Subjects: LCSH: Children's songs, English—United States—Texts. | CYAC: Dinosaurs—Songs and music. | Songs.

Classification: LCC PZ8.3.B4558 We 2017 | DDC 782.42—dc23

LC record available at http://lccn.loc.gov/2015032132

LAURIE BERKNER
WE ARE THE DINOSAURS

ILLUSTRATED BY BEN CLANTON

Simon & Schuster Books for Young Readers
New York London Toronto Sydney New Delhi

We are the dinosaurs,

Let's go, Dax!

marching, marching.
We are the dinosaurs—
WHADDAYA THINK OF THAT?

We are the dinosaurs,
marching, marching.
We are the dinosaurs.

We make the earth flat.

We make the earth flat.

We stop and eat our food
on the ground.

We stop and eat our food

when we're in the mood.
We stop and eat our food,

we are the dinosaurs,
marching, marching.

We are the dinosaurs,
marching, marching.
We are the dinosaurs.
We make the earth flat.
We make the earth flat.

We stop and take a rest
over in our nest.
We stop and take a rest
at the end of the day.

We are the dinosaurs, marching, marching.
We are the dinosaurs—WHADDAYA THINK OF THAT? We are the dinosaurs, marching, marching.

We are the dinosaurs.

We make the earth flat.

Why . . . ?

Because we are the dinosaurs!

ROOAARRR!

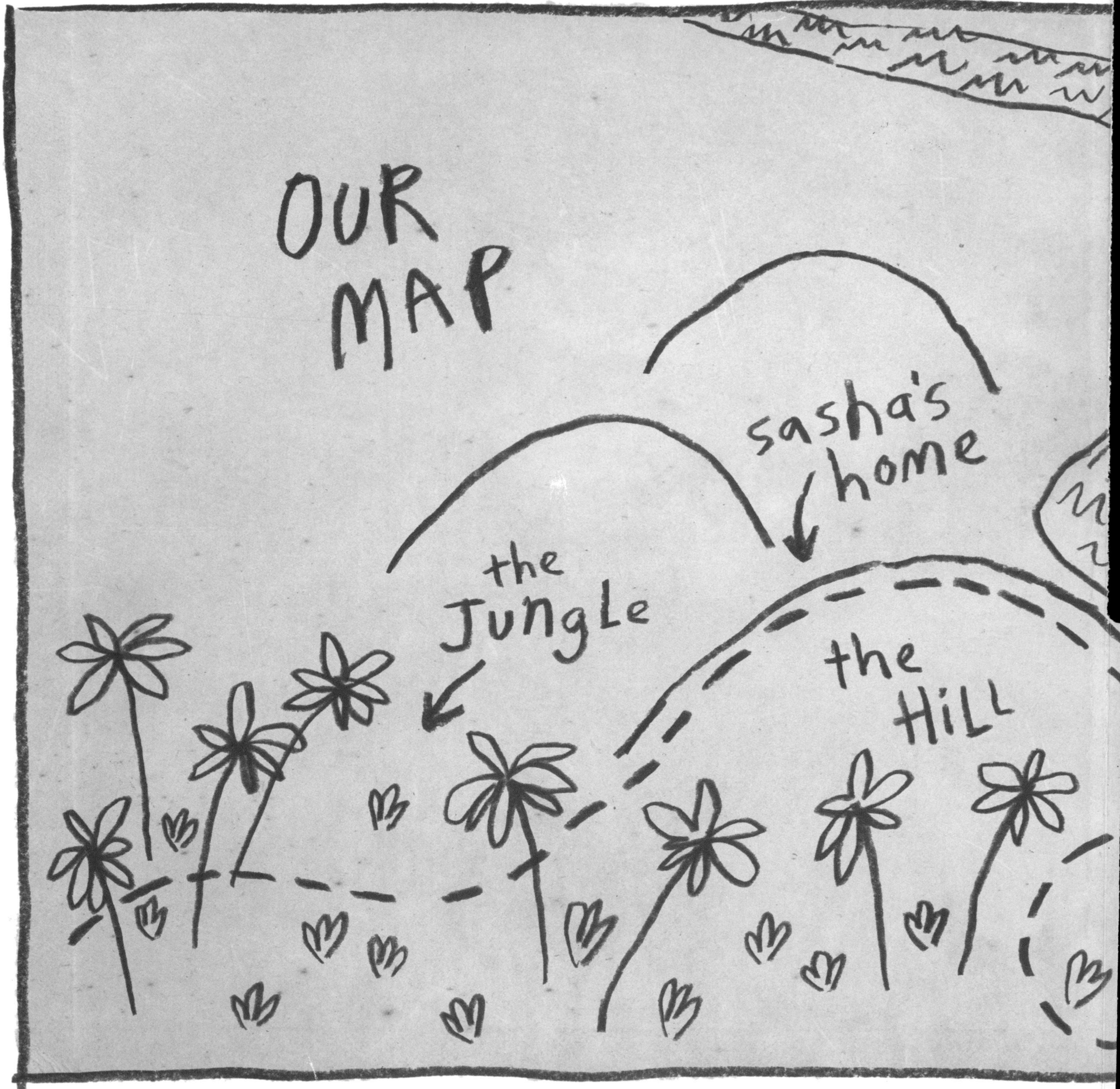
OUR MAP
sasha's home
the Jungle
the HiLL